raining cats and dogs   fliuch

báisteach   wet day   the rain is waiting

lashing   bucketing   drizzle

pouring   pelting   splashing

soft   misting

pelting   slating down

thunder   spitting

fliuch

hammering

dripping

wetting

sunshower   enough rain

arriving   local rain

fierce   soft day

ra...   ...ogs   fliuch

Eva and the
Perfect Rain

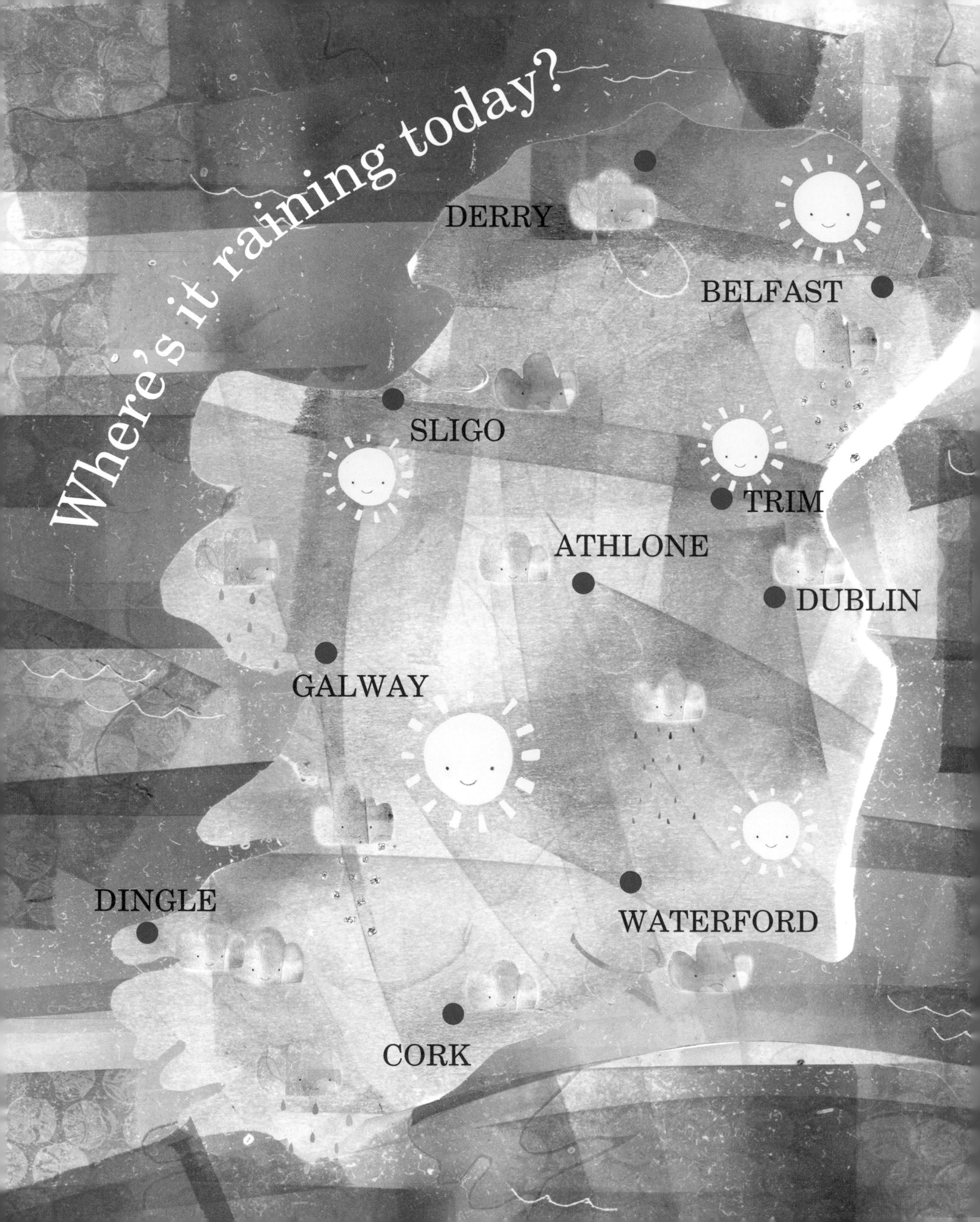

Where's it raining today?

DERRY

BELFAST

SLIGO

TRIM

ATHLONE

DUBLIN

GALWAY

DINGLE

WATERFORD

CORK

Eva and the Perfect Rain

A Rainy Irish Tale

Tatyana Feeney

THE O'BRIEN PRESS
DUBLIN

When Eva woke up, she looked outside
and saw it was raining

– again!

She couldn't wait to go outside
with her **new umbrella**!

But her dad called her
back for breakfast.

And before she had finished eating,
the rain turned **thundery**
so she had to stay inside.

When the thunder stopped Eva rushed outside with her umbrella...
but the rain was **so soft** that she didn't need her umbrella at all.

Instead, she found a nice, deep puddle, just right for splashing.

Maybe if she jumped hard enough **a fish**... or **a dolphin**... or even **a mermaid** would come out!

Tired of jumping,
Eva looked straight up
into the clouds.

She felt the rain
landing gently on
her face.

This rain was lovely,

but it just **wasn't** perfect umbrella rain…

13

Suddenly, the rain began to **pour** down.

This must be the **perfect rain**!

14

Eva ran to get her
new umbrella, but
the wind blew the
rain sideways and even with
her umbrella she still got wet.

15

The wind was so **strong**!

It caught Eva's umbrella and pulled her along.

She pretended she was flying!

A **gust** tore Eva's umbrella
out of her hands and down the road.

Oh no!

She thought it might be lost forever!

But she found it next door in a tree.
Eva decided this **wasn't** perfect
umbrella weather and they
both went inside.

When the wind died down, the rain became a **drizzle**,

finally **just right** for taking a walk with her new umbrella.

Eva stopped, nice and dry, and watched the drip drops filling up her puddle.

All the rain had made
the colours **brighter**.

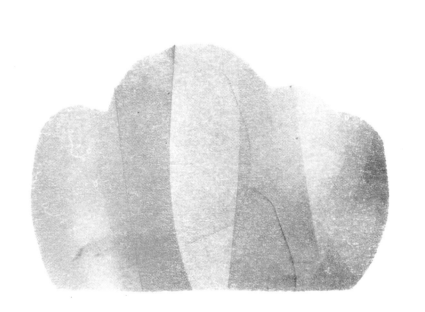

When Eva reached the end of her road the **sun** came out.

Rain was still falling –
it was a **sun shower**!

A **rainbow**
stretched across
the sky...

...and made it the most **perfect rain** of all.

TATYANA FEENEY grew up in North Carolina, where she spent much of her childhood reading and drawing. This developed into a love of art and particularly illustrations in children's books.

Tatyana now lives in Co. Meath with her husband and two children. She has illustrated several books in the O'Brien Press Panda series and is also the author and illustrator of *Socks for Mr Wolf*, for The O'Brien Press, as well as *Small Bunny's Blue Blanket*, *Little Owl's Orange Scarf*, *Little Frog's Tadpole Trouble* and *Small Elephant's Bathtime*.

To Corinne, 'Ain't it good to know you've got a friend?'

First published 2019 by The O'Brien Press Ltd,
12 Terenure Road East, Rathgar, Dublin 6, D06 HD27, Ireland
Tel: +353 1 4923333; Fax: +353 1 4922777
E-mail: books@obrien.ie
Website: www.obrien.ie
The O'Brien Press is a member of Publishing Ireland.

Published in

DUBLIN
UNESCO
City of Literature

ISBN: 978-1-84717-978-4

6 5 4 3 2 1
21 20 19

Printed and bound in Poland by Białostockie Zakłady Graficzne S.A.
The paper in this book is produced using pulp from managed forests.

Eva and the Perfect Rain receives financial assistance from the Arts Council